BRIGHT BURSTS OF COLOUR

D1342931

BLOOMSBURY EDUCATION
Bloomsbury Publishing Plc
50 Bedford Square, London, WC1B 3DP, UK
29 Earlsfort Terrace, Dublin 2, Ireland

BLOOMSBURY, BLOOMSBURY EDUCATION and the Diana logo are trademarks of
Bloomsbury Publishing Plc

First published in Great Britain in 2020 by Bloomsbury Publishing Plc
Text copyright © Matt Goodfellow, 2020
Illustrations copyright © Aleksei Bitskoff, 2020

Matt Goodfellow and Aleksei Bitskoff have asserted their rights under the Copyright,
Designs and Patents Act, 1988, to be identified as Author and Illustrator of this work

A catalogue record for this book is available from the British Library

ISBN: PB: 978-1-4729-6354-3; ePDF: 978-1-4729-6353-6; ePub: 978-1-4729-6355-0

4 6 8 10 9 7 5

Text design by Cathy Tincknell
Printed and bound by CPI Group (UK) Ltd, Croydon, CR0 4YY

To find out more about our authors and books visit www.bloomsbury.com
and sign up for our newsletters

BRIGHT BURSTS OF COLOUR

Poems by
Matt Goodfellow

Illustrated by
Aleksei Bitskoff

BLOOMSBURY EDUCATION
LONDON OXFORD NEW YORK NEW DELHI SYDNEY

*For all who change the world
with kindness*

Contents

The Sometimes Song

sometimes in the shadows
sometimes in the light
sometimes when it's cloudy
sometimes when it's bright

sometimes when it seems like
darkness might have won
we sometimes sing the sometimes song
the one we sang with Mum

Poetry

poetry in motion:
elegant and smooth

poetry commotion:
noisy, loud, rude

poetry in potion:
magic from a cup

poetry promotion:
words are goin' up

poetry in ocean:
salty, cold, drippy

poetry in lotion:
dangerously slippy

poetry emotion:
pull yourself together

poetry devotion:
in our hearts forever

Missing Lessons

New year's first frost tightens my cheeks
as I walk with Mum through town's
stretching streets.

I'm missing morning lessons
to see the doctor
again.

Two teenagers tut and grumble,
one hops from foot to foot
as they wait for a shop to open.

A whistling window-cleaner
lobs his sponge into a bucket,
winks at me as we pass.

Men in yellow vests
sip coffee outside a café and laugh
talking in loud, rough voices.

An old lady, thin as her stick
dabs red-rimmed eyes with a tissue.
Shutters clank.

A train rumbles the pavement.
And it's like I'm the only one
who's been let backstage.

And for the first time, I get it:
how it works
how it all fits together.

And Mum hurries on ahead
worrying about what the doctor said
last time –
what he'll say today.

But back here
I see the world

and I know its secrets.

If Cats had Flavoured Fur

If cats had flavoured fur
it'd surely make all those
time-consuming grooming sessions
much more enjoyable.

Take my cat, Jessie, for example –
she's a tortoiseshell:
white, ginger and brown.
Currently, each patch of fur
must taste the same: furry.
Boring.

Now
if cats had flavoured fur
the white bits could taste of, say,
milk instead – mmm!
Far more pleasurable for her.
Nice cold, ice cold milk.
Refreshing.

If cats had flavoured fur
Jessie's ginger bits would have to taste of
ginger.
I don't know if Jessie likes
ginger.
Or if cats in general like
ginger.
But they'd have to taste of ginger.
It's my poem, so end of.

If cats had flavoured fur
what could Jessie's brown bits be?
Sausages? Possibly.
Chicken skin? Hmm.
Both a bit rich for Jessie's simple tastes,
I imagine.
How about biscuits? Cat biscuits. Yes!
She likes those.
Crunchy cat biscuits
cracking on her back teeth.

Sorted.

Milk, ginger and cat biscuits.
I'm pretty certain she'd like that.

Yes,
surely she'd prefer
to be a cat
with flavoured fur.

Ten

The kitchen table's
heart beats
alive
with party pulse.

I take a deep breath
blow out
ten bright candles

give Mum, Dad
Grandma
a kiss

and make my
wish

to always remember
being here
today

like this.

Chameleon Kids

chameleon kids are elusive
their skill is to rarely be found
drifting through days undetected
blending with those they're around

chameleon kids are careful
their secrets are never revealed
camouflage acting as armour
means feelings are safely concealed

some of them yearn to burn brightly
but predators lurk everywhere
so they learn to disguise any fire in their eyes
until not even *they* know it's there

Hot Stuff

I swallowed the sun
to see what I'd learn.
The lesson it taught:
Don't. It'll burn.

Split

I stay at Mum's for half the week
the other half at Dad's.
Both of them re-married
to people not that bad.

I've got a baby sister
she looks like me they say.
When I'm at my dad's, I miss her –
she changes every day.

Mum picks me up from Dad's house
but never rings the bell:
it makes her sad to see him –
she won't say but I can tell.

Rules are really different
to be honest, it's a pain –
I can tell you've been at his house –
Dad says just the same.

I've got some mates to chill with
but I'm only here part time –
they've got mates they're tighter with
and I don't mind, it's fine.

The 'steps' don't do that much with me
but say they want me there –
still I always get the feeling
they're glad I'm out their hair.

I don't detest this life of mine
but wish I could've had
a chance to see what things were like
just me and Mum and Dad.

They did the best they could, I s'pose
the rest is out their hands.
I've tried to talk about it
but no one understands.

They see a clever, cocky kid
expensive bike and phone
two happy loving houses –
when all I want's a home

Mist

I don't know
what it is
about mist
that makes me
walk early
by the river
and wrap myself
in its delicate
embrace

ah, but I
think I'm lying
to myself again
I *do* know
what it is
and it's this:
sometimes
if the light
is just right
I can
still see
your face

A Special Badger

I'm a special kind of badger
in a special badger den
writing special badger poems
with a special badger pen
learning special badger lessons
in a special badger school
earning special badger kudos
for my special badger cool
wearing special badger badges
saying *badgers are the best*
passing special badger interviews
and special badger tests
drinking special badger coffee
from a special badger mug
but my special badger problem:

I am actually a slug

Just Words

I tasted a word: fiery, hot
loosened a word from a fisherman's knot
fattened a word on saucers of cream
quarried a word, got rich on its seam

planted a word deep in the soil
anointed a word with ashes and oil
harnessed a word, exploited its power
banished a word to an ivory tower

polished a word, wore it pinned to my chest
finished a word with a rattling breath

Doggy

my faithful doggy loves a stroke
when curled up on my bed

he loves his tummy tickled
and a gently patted head

he loves to roll in smelly things
he loves to chew a stick

he knows when I am feeling sad
and gives my face a lick

he cheers me up, he makes me laugh
he loves a muddy walk

he tilts his little head to me
and listens when I talk

I've taught him how to give high–fives
to sit, and walk to heel

my faithful dog, my greatest friend:
if only you were real

Liam

Last year
this lad joined our class.
He'd been to loads of different schools
up and down the country
following where his dad's work was.

He said he liked it,
moving around,
that it kept things alive
and interesting.

One time
at break
he told me he was
different

that his thoughts
were bright bursts
of colour
greens and reds
blues and golds
all moving together –

said they were so bright
they sometimes hurt his eyes.

He's gone now, of course,
was only here a month or so.

But every now and then
I picture him
standing at the edge
of some playground

and I wonder if he's nervous,
if he ever feels afraid
that staying in a place too long
might make
the colours
fade.

Goggles

got my goggles on
heading straight to the pool
got my goggles on
looking sharp, feeling cool
got my goggles on
but they feel a little tight
got my goggles on
neither eye is working right
got my goggles on
trip and fall into the pool
got my goggles on
feel exactly like a fool
got my goggles on
clamber out, splutter, cough
had my goggles on
took my stupid goggles off

Trapped

I am
a ship

this classroom
the bottle

that keeps my
sails sagged

the clock ticks
until three

when Miss opens
the door –

lets in
the wind

Just Enough

just a feather of a thought
but enough to see me through

just a feather of a thought
and I line my nest with you

Inside

inside a vase
there are miniature cars
driving in circles for hours

though progress is slow
(for there's nowhere to go)
they've a wonderful view of the flowers

Fledgling

(For the staff and pupils of All Saints Primary, Gorton, Manchester)

the ball is picked up
as stooping to look
four boys point
at the crooked little fledgling thrush
crouched against the fence

look, sir
look
a bird, sir
a baby bird
it's frightened
poor thing
what can we do, sir?

dark chest-speckles heave
as it hops
scuff-footed across the gravel
playground

makes a stuttering
flap-dart
angling into the low branches
of a sycamore

the boys stand

shadows
beneath
a low sun

a shout
shatters

come on
come on
enough of the fuss

five minutes to go

and it's
2–1 to us

David

David could draw the most beautiful planes I
        ever saw:

didn't need a ruler to get the lines straight
designs of blue-sky genius from a mind only eight.

At playtime we became them: supersonic jets
blasting though the atmosphere, both our arms
        outstretched.

He taught me how to sketch, and told me mine were
        good.
When I said I couldn't do it, he showed me that I
        could.

Then David's mum met someone new – he had to
        move away
packed up all his pictures, emptied out his tray.

Every flight was cancelled, every drawing gone.
I walked around for weeks: forgotten, lost, numb.

Until it all came back to me: that look in David's eye
I raised my arms, ran – and remembered how to fly.

Believe

when
Wilbur
and Orville
promised us
flight

the doubters were many

but the
brothers
were
Wright

Wilbur and Orville Wright are generally credited with inventing, building, and flying the world's first successful aeroplane.

Ghost on the Glass

Mr Weston said it was probably a pigeon because
    there's always loads of them
hanging around the playground – it must've seen
    the field's reflection
in our classroom window and thought it was flying
    towards it.

Happens quite a lot, he said – the bird would
    probably be fine, just a headache.
But I wasn't so sure. The same thing happened at
    our house a few years ago
when we were having tea:

a bang on the kitchen window sent us outside to
    find a tiny, perfect goldfinch lying on
the patio, feet to the sky. Dad said most birds that
    hit windows died – if not straight
away, pretty soon afterwards.

In class, I couldn't finish my story, didn't care about
    science or maths.
Just kept thinking about that pigeon
    and its ghost left on the glass.

Book People

they
lie disguised in margins
hide   where spines crack

slender limbs
like letters
glisten   tight
black

make
silent pink-eyed promises
of love   death
trust

disturbed by page vibrations

disappear to

dust

Four Seasons in One Class

Autumn's an enigma
radiant but cool
catwalks down the corridor
decorates the school

Winter's work is surgical
crisp in all her books
precise with polar pleasantries
dispatches distant looks

Spring enriches everyone
nourishes the room
every day she finds a way
to make her table bloom

Summer stretches out each task
finger-twists blonde hair
consultant of the calendar
each holiday a prayer

I Fell in Love with a Crumpet

I fell in love with a crumpet: its crispy, cratered skin
called to me one morning, sucked my poor heart in.

I carried it around with me safe inside my pocket
until I'd finished fashioning a crumpet-carrying locket

which hung around my slender neck just like a
    buttered moon –
a medal won by sweet new love. Yet tragedy came
    soon.

I thought we'd stay together until we both were old
but hadn't factored in a crumpet's tendency to mould.

The stench became unbearable: a green and gassy
glow
told me it was time I had to let my true love go.

I buried it in dappled shade beneath a willow tree
and wondered how I might survive a life of only me.

But have no fear, I'm not the sort to end up sad
and bitter
and six days later hit it off with a gorgeous
wholemeal pitta.

Assembly

(In memory of Joan Cullen: a special teacher and friend)

the old hall floor
is cold this morning
as we settle down to
sit
sleet–streaked hair
stuck to scalps

the teachers shush
and hush
fingers to lips

when the shuffling
stops
Miss Cullen's smile
welcomes us

the music starts

and we warm ourselves
at the fire

of song

Catch Her if You Can

winter–thin
hard as hills
smooth as silver
pale as pills
dream–like where the starlight spills
catch her if you can

no clear edges
moves like smoke
leads you blindly
like a joke
through black trees that squeeze and choke
catch her if you can

follow follow
slip and twist
grasping air
in empty fist
wonder wonder what you missed
catch her if you can

Happy

this morning I just wondered
will it always be like this

footsteps blacken frozen grass
schoolbags at our hips

biker-boys come charging past
blow the girls a kiss

this morning I just wondered
will it always be like this

I Will Sing

I've spent
a long time
listening

catching words
that slip
from lips
and stick
to my hair
my clothes

my skin

I've collected
each unit
of sound
each feeling

kept them close
for the day
when

I will sing

Grandpa's Shoes

Grandpa's shoes
laced up tight

Grandpa's shoes
clean and bright

Grandpa's shoes
small and neat

Grandpa's shoes
without grandpa's feet

The Shortest Ever Secondary School Career

High school

Bye school

Where We Shouldn't Be

the pond isn't safe
they say

the woods
too dangerous
for exploring
or play

but here
where we walk
in the dark air
of day

it is only
a blackbird
that gives us
away

Wonder Watcher

I lie in bed, staring at the ceiling
allow my mind to wander where it will
I capture certain thoughts, special feelings
let concentration hold them close and still
then suddenly, like dust in sunlit air
I close my eyes to find that words are there

I stand within our playground's swirling noise
and step through strobing shadows into light
I weave between the giddy groups of boys
believing I can memorise each sight
then back in class when settled in my chair
I close my eyes to find that words are there

I worry that one day I might not see
if all my time gets filled with grown-up strife
yet hope that I'm the thing I'll always be:
a wonder watcher wandering through life
discovering amazement everywhere
closing eyes to find that words are there

Dogs with Human Names

Dogs with human names
really make me laugh:
Graham's licking granny's foot!
Oh, Dave, you need a bath!

Dogs with human names
make me howl so I can't breathe:
Elspeth's had an accident!
Goodness, Peter, please!

Dogs with human names
make me double up and giggle:
Stop it, Mr Stephenson,
you needle when you nibble!

Agatha to Andy
Jennifer to James
I think they're great, let's celebrate
dogs with human names!

Too Late

it is
late

no-light-slice-under-door
late

Max-in-kitchen-basket-chin-on-paws
late

the glass is cold
against my forehead

so much black
there

so much

night

Brum Brum

Dad bought maps of the stars
but says he'll be returning 'em:

we were supposed to get to Mars
but ended up in Birmingham

The Not a Poem Poem

I am not
a poem

no I'm not like that at all

I am not
a poem

unconventional and small

I am not
a poem

let's be absolutely clear

I am not
a poem

there is not a poem here

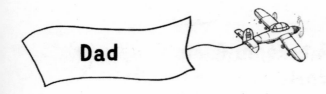

Dad

Dad used to laugh when I told him a joke,
sit down and listen whenever I spoke.

Dad used to read me a story each night,
give me a kiss as he turned out the light.

Dad used to play in the garden with me,
A quick game of footy then in for our tea.

Lately he doesn't have time for our fun,
home late from work and just argues with Mum.

It's like he's forgotten that he has a son —
I just wish I knew what it is that I've done.

The Greatest Play in the World

a
single
act

of kindness

Archie's Getting Old

he used to be a regal beagle
advancing years left him feeble
got mugged off by a streetwise seagull
Archie's getting old

more Rip Van Winkle than Evil Knievel
cares no more for tom-cat needle
had his fill of all upheaval
Archie's getting old

no more barks or ball-retrieval
close your eyes my grey-beard treacle
walk in woodland soft and peaceful
Archie's getting old

Rip Van Winkle is a character from a story who
fell asleep for twenty years.
Evil Kneivel was a famous American daredevil
who did crazy things on motorbikes.

Difficult

I can be the classroom joker
laughter flowing easily
I can charge along the corridor
surging like the sea
I can be the crazy brave one
swinging wildly from a tree
but why is it so difficult
for me to just be me?

I can chat about the weekend
ask you what you had for tea
I can spiral round the playground
easy-going, worry-free
I can spend each day beside you
and never let you see
that sometimes it's so difficult
for me to just be me

Strest

Charlie never cries,

not even
when he came down the slide
too fast in Year 5
and broke his wrist.
Miss couldn't believe it;
he even smiled and waved
to our class across the playground
when Mr Smith drove him off
to hospital.

Charlie never cries,

not even
when his gran died –
he was back in school
the next day
said he was fine,
he'd survive –
but you could see it
in the shadows
of his eyes.

Charlie never cries

but when it was time
for the reading paper

we'd
revised
revised
revised
for,
Charlie sighed
flicked through the pages
for ages
put his pen down.
Miss appeared at his side
saying, *try your best, Charlie*
it's just a test, Charlie
and he looked over at me
and I swear I could see
right inside his mind
and it was dark
and he was hiding
shoulders shaking
and he knew
he couldn't do
what they wanted
him to do
however hard he tried.

And I'll never forget
the day of the test,

the day
Charlie
cried.

All Things Must Pass

except me

I guard my precious
jealously

dummy, dribble, pirouette

curl it
chip it
burst the net

a hat-trick-hitting deity

all things must pass

all things

but

me

ExPEARiment

we hoped when poached
its flesh'd be better

a bitter conclusion:
still minging, just wetter

The Day

We cycle over beech nuts.
He points out our breath,
columns of sunlight
shining through the changing trees
and the damp-heavy river smell.
I'm worried about today's
spelling and times table tests –
I struggle with *witch* and *which*.
We practise my sixes and eights
as we pedal past cloudy-faced kids
and parents.
He helps me across
the busy road, laughs at the
grumpy caretaker who sighs
and swings his keys as he lets the morning masses
pass through the gates.
I put my bike
in the bike shed.
He kisses me
tells me not to worry about stuff.
I love you, have a good day
see you later, kidda, I'll be here
at half three. Good luck.

I wave through the window
as overhead a plane is coming into land.
He pushes his bike through playground puddles
and turns to blow me one last kiss.
Puts on his helmet and adjusts the strap.

And it's five years later
and he never came back.

The Clouded House

The Clouded House has many different rooms
    for you to visit
open doors, go in, explore –
they're special and exquisite:

the thunder room
is restless
rattles brick and joist
in order to express this:
power has a voice

the room of snow
sparkles
takes you in its arms
settle down beneath the stars
far away from harm

the hailstone room
has rhythm
pounding from the sky
each snare-drum snap a pistol crack
a cold defiant cry

the room of rain
changes
a thousand times an hour
delicious desert deluge

to brutal Baltic shower

one more door
is all that's left
I'm waiting there for you
through the gloom
my favourite room:
sunlight breaking through

BREAKfast

a bowl o' granola
bust holes in a molar –
this message I'll spread
as I travel:

you don't need to eat
something just 'cos it's sweet
for it may have the texture
of gravel

Better at Yours

we can't go to my house, Dad's still in bed
black-eyes and beer cans pounding his head
I swear if you saw him you'd think he was dead –
I like it better at yours

another time, maybe, the place is a mess
Mum's at my auntie's, *'dealing with stress'*
we need peace and quiet to revise for this test –
I like it better at yours

I like how it smells and the biscuits you've got
there's bread in the cupboards and tea in the pot
carpets are clean and the radiator's hot –
I like it better at yours

Ride

I   like
my   bike

the
whirring blur
of churning cogs
turns worlds
beneath
my feet

into something
separate

from me

that
I can't
feel
or see

I   like
my   bike

I am

free

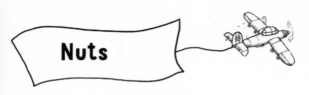

Nuts

I wouldn't want a burger or a curry or a quiche
I wouldn't push a pasty past my lips and tongue and
    teeth
I'd hate to have a thousand things all swimming in my
    guts
'cos I was born a squirrel, so it's: NUTS! NUTS! NUTS!

variety anxiety is not what squirrels do
we don't want sausage sandwiches or chunky chicken
    stew
no jelly-pots that wobble like your big fat human butts
'cos I was born a squirrel, so it's: NUTS! NUTS! NUTS!

when I'm in your garden stealing peanuts from the
    birds
take on board my reasoning, it's truthful, not absurd
don't shake a fist or do me down with disappointed
    tuts –
remember I'm a squirrel, so it's: NUTS! NUTS! NUTS!

Broken

I wish mum's phone
was broken

battered
beaten
smashed

I wish mum's phone
was broken

maybe then she'd ask:

why my friends have vanished
and my uniform's a state
why I leave for school on time
but always get there late

why I turn away if someone
asks how I am coping

I
really
really
really
really

wish mum's phone
was broken

The Sky is the Colour of Grandma's Hair

The sky is the colour
of Grandma's hair

and puts me in mind
of times with her:

tents in the garden
wellies, mud

listening eyes
that just understood.

Rain's falling heavy
I really don't care.

The sky is the colour
of Grandma's hair.

Empty

we
took her clothes
to the charity shop
this morning
like she wanted
us to

now
I'm sitting inside
her wardrobe
holding my knees

and somehow
I know
that wherever I travel
however old I get

there will
always be
a part of me
sitting right
here

Chester Zoo

The news report said there'd been a fire.
Most animals were safe
but *a small number of species were lost.*
Things I'd never heard of before:
cinnamon frogs
tentacled snakes
grosbeak starlings.
It said keepers guided six orangutans
away from the flames
by tempting them with bananas.

And as I lie here in bed
I'm thinking about those orangutans
and how strange it must be
to have lived their entire lives
in captivity

only now to learn
what it feels like to be wild

by watching their world burn.

socks socks socks
socks socks socks
socks socks socks
socks socks socks socks
socks socks socks socks
socks socks socks socks
socks socks socks
socks socks socks

socks
socks socks socks
socks socks socks socks
socks

socks
socks socks socks socks
socks socks socks socks
socks socks socks socks
socks socks socks socks socks
socks socks socks socks
socks socks socks socks socks
socks socks socks socks socks
socks socks socks socks socks
socks socks socks socks socks
socks socks socks socks socks socks
socks socks socks socks socks
socks socks socks socks socks
socks socks socks socks
socks socks socks socks

79

Cheers

every now and then
Dad says
come on lad
none of that healthy-eating stuff tonight
forget the broccoli
put the salad away
we're having burgers for tea

and we walk to the takeaway
at the end of the road

the one where the windows
are always steamed up

where the men
talk quickly in voices
I don't understand

where burgers
are pressed to sizzling black bars
by metal tongues

where change clatters
on the counter and the man
calls us *my friends*

walking home
Dad swings the bag
and whistles

he sits opposite me
at the table

we snap our coke cans
open at the same time

touch them together

he winks

cheers, son

cheers, Dad

When the Mask Slips

they don't happen often anymore
the mad minutes
when the mask slips

but I love it when
they do

kitten again
she skids across the laminate floor
in the kitchen
batting Mum's handbag straps
like they're alive

charges out the back door

scuds full pelt across the garden
diving at leaves
grass snapping

then stops
dead

licks her paws

remembers

slips the mask
back on

Child Soldiers

faces speak of battle
scars of savage wars
eyes of empty sadness
lost innocence has caused

guns speak for their masters
knives for blinkered hate
silence for compliance
resigned to no escape

they dream of education
peaceful life desire
but morning shouts its warning
to lift their guns and fire

hearts sing of their villages
of family by the door
of football pitches etched in dirt
of shooting just to score

There (a refugee song)

Where roads run out
and quiet winds blow
far from fences
that's where we'll go.

Where blossom falls freely
like warm summer snow
and leaves sing of sunlight
that's where we'll go.

Where no one will find us
and no one will know
safe in the silence
that's where we'll go.

Somewhere, a Sister

maybe the same eyes
as her father

walks like him
smiles like him

I wonder
if we met

would we recognise
each other

look without doubt
into the eyes

of our
mother

Ghost Walk

Our guide is tall and pale as whalebones.
A thin cane in his hand, black top hat and
long black leather jacket. He folds

ticket–price tens and twenties into
the pocket of black combat pants tucked
into black boots. We walk down alleyways

and narrow streets; hear tales of lost sailors,
jilted maidens; see mansions of whaling–ship
owners who made and lost fortunes. We applaud

the final story. He bows and smiles. I watch him
walk back to his black car, take off his jacket
and hat, open the boot and pack his ghosts away.

Bram

From this Whitby harbour bench
I see a dog
black as smokehouse eaves
break free
from the shipwreck's belly
and lurch up
church steps.

Across the cliffs
its gleaming eyes
challenge me to believe

until it leaps
across howling air
into my mind

and then

flows through my veins
and out of
my pen.

Bram Stoker was the author of Dracula. The story is set in Whitby and the main character, a vampire, escapes from a shipwreck, coming ashore in the form of a black dog.

Still Aloud

the magical minutes
that finish our day:

gather together
Miss Davies will say

lessons are over
now what we need

is freedom
and wonder

sit down

I will read

Hot

it is hot
so hot in class

we are trapped
behind this glass

and it's hot
too hot to talk

and it's hot
too hot to mess

and it's hot
too hot to walk

and it's hot
too hot for tests

and it's hot
too hot to read

and it's hot
too hot to laugh

and it's hot
too hot to breathe

it is hot
so hot in class

Remember

when shadows creep across your mind
and smiles are thin and tight
when you do what you believe in
but question if it's right
when you focus not on what you've got
but all the things you lack
there may be rain at the front of the house
but sunshine round the back

when you can't remember where you found
the words you used to say
when your heartbeat is the music
that you listen to each day
when you turn away from talent
in case you lose the knack
there may be rain at the front of the house
but sunshine round the back

Acknowledgements

'Chameleon Kids' first published in Poetry for a Change: A National Poetry Day Anthology, Otter-Barry Books (2018); 'Fledgling' first published in The Caterpillar, Issue 22 (Autumn 2018).
All poems © Matt Goodfellow.